The Sc...

Mary Hooper

ALFORD PRIMARY SCHOOL

Illustrated by Liz Roberts

CHAPTER ONE

It was a Friday afternoon and we'd all
been doing circuits of the gym equipment
for ages and ages. Well, the others had; *I'd*
been trekking round the outside trying to
look fully occupied, but actually not
doing anything at all. I was just going
round for the umpteenth time and
wondering whether, if I trekked right out

of the doors, anyone would notice, when Mr Ward, our PE teacher, suddenly clapped his hands and yelled for silence.

He stood at the front of the hall, big and square and looming over everyone. His nickname wasn't Wardrobe for nothing.

"And now the details you've all been waiting for!" Wardrobe announced. "The splendid, stupendous, scintillating and startling – School Trip!"

All around me the class broke into cheers while I slunk against the radiator. School trip! As if *going* to the school wasn't bad enough without going on a *trip* with them...

"Now, you've seen the photos taken in other years so you'll know what's expected of you – and if I were you I should start getting terrified right now!" He gave a wicked laugh. "After a week at

Tarbeck Gorge even your own mothers won't recognise you!"

I shuddered. I hated outdoors-ish things and felt positively *sick* at the idea of games, so I'd got pretty good at forging *"Would you please excuse Jane..."* letters from home at my old school. This school trip – well, I *had* seen the photos outside the Head's office, and it looked a nightmare. Like a load of gym lessons strung together. Hours and *hours* of them.

Everyone in my class – 10A – broke into excited chatter, but I just measured the distance to the door. The minute the bell rang I was going to bolt towards the changing rooms. With a bit of luck I'd be able to run straight into the showers and out again without getting wet.

"Quiet!" Wardrobe boomed. "Now, to start with – on this totally terrifying trip you'll be sleeping in single-sex dorms, and beds will be allocated in strictly alphabetical order, so it's no use asking to be next to your best friend."

I stared out of the window. I didn't *have* a best friend. I hardly had any friends at all at Ridgeway Primary – I'd only been there two weeks. There was just Fiona; she was the nearest thing because when I'd started she'd been the only one to bother to speak to me. She was quite clever and a lot quieter than me – but then *I'd* turned out to be pretty quiet at this school.

Wardrobe rubbed his hands; the noise was like two sheets of sandpaper sliding together. "Those of you with older brothers and sisters who went on the trip..." he gave a dark laugh, "...those with brothers or sisters who came back in one piece, I should say, will know what we get up to there, but if any of you *don't*, let me tell you that it's dangerous, devilish and dastardly stuff."

"Great!" shouted Speedy King, the most obnoxious boy in 10A, jumping up and down. "What'll we do there, sir?"

"Well, a typical day might be an early start – four o'clock in the morning – with a long-distance run through the forest."

"Will we need special shoes, sir?" Speedy asked.

"Certainly not!" Wardrobe said. "Shoes indeed! Shoes are for sissies."

There was an appreciative "Yeah!" from some of the class.

"We come back at seven for an ice-cold shower under the waterfall."

"And then do we get breakfast?" Speedy's mate Tigger interrupted.

"Breakfast! What's breakfast?" roared Wardrobe. "You might get a dry biscuit at eleven o'clock if you're lucky – that's if you're back from swimming across the gorge with a rucksack on your head. And then only if none of your kit has got wet."

I shuddered, and put up my hand. "What... what if you can't swim, sir?" I asked.

"Oh, don't worry about that, Jane," he said. "We just chuck you in the deep bit – you'll soon learn."

Everyone sniggered and I looked at them coldly. *Oh, great...*

"And what after that, sir?" Speedy asked.

"After we've chucked Jane in?" Wardrobe said jovially.

"No – after we're back from swimming across the gorge," Speedy said.

"Well, then you can choose between abseiling down a cliff face or paragliding from the mountain top – or alternatively you could leap off the bridge holding on to a long bit of elastic."

The class murmured excitedly, giggled and nudged each other. I nearly passed out.

"Whatever you choose to do you're fully insured," Wardrobe went on. "The centre is equipped with an emergency surgery and X-ray unit, and wooden crutches and wheelchairs are given away entirely free."

"Wow!" went several of the boys. Wardrobe beat his chest. He often did this; he thought he was Tarzan. "Yes, a week at Tarbeck Gorge will sort the men from the boys!" he said. He looked round

uneasily – Ms Williams, our class tutor, was pretty hot on statements like that.

"And... er... the women from the girls," he added.

"Cor... it'll be like Indiana Jones!" Tigger called.

"*Indiana Jones!*" Wardrobe puffed out his cheeks and made a *pshaw* sort of noise. "I'd eat him for breakfast. Let me tell you it's going to be a *lot* more dangerous than that!"

"Yeah!" Speedy and Tigger yelled, punching the air.

"And all you have to do is take one of these forms and ask a parent to fill it in. Collect it from me on your way to the shower," he finished, just as the bell rang.

I didn't feel like bolting into the changing rooms then – I was too horrified to bolt anywhere. All I could manage to do was go up to Wardrobe on shaky legs and ask if we *had* to go.

"Of course!" he said bracingly, pushing a form into my hand. "What's up – can't swim? I told you, we..."

"I know, sir," I said. "But I don't like it outdoors. I don't like the cold. I'll catch flu. And I can't run and I hate cold showers and..."

He gave a great laugh and clapped me on the shoulder so hard that I flew across to the wall bars. "Nonsense!" he said. "Be the making of you. Too namby-pamby by half, some of you lot!"

"But..."

"A ten-mile midnight hike walking on your hands is just what you could do with!"

His next class ran in then, whooping and calling and generally being jolly and active, and I slunk away.

Outside the gym, Fiona was waiting for me. She was clutching her shoe bag and was as neat and tidy as usual. She looked quite ordinary, quite *calm*.

I stared at her. "How can you just stand there smiling?" I asked. "Doesn't it sound *awful!* You're not going, are you?"

"What – on the trip?" she said. She shrugged. "You've got to go; it's compulsory. In their last term here everyone goes to Tarbeck Gorge."

"Everyone except *me*," I said.

CHAPTER TWO

I left Fiona in the High Street and walked home. I say home, but it wasn't really. Home was near Salisbury, which was 120 miles away, but I was living with my gran for a year while my dad carried out some special contract in the Middle East. My sister Georgina was at university so *she* hadn't had to move, and although Mum had gone to the Middle East with Dad they didn't think it was suitable for me because of schools and things.

I kicked a can along the street miserably. How come it was suitable for me to leave all my friends at school in Salisbury and come here, then? Here to a horrible big rough school where everyone played football and you were forced to go on school trips devised specially to kill you. I sighed; what I'd give to be back in Salisbury, with Manveer and Mandy and everyone. We'd had a right laugh...

I rang the bell and Gran answered, beaming round the door at me. "Hello, dear! Good day?"

"Awful," I said.

"That's nice." I rolled my eyes; I sometimes got the distinct impression that she didn't listen to what I said.

"Now, I've made caraway seed buns and nutty flapjacks..."

I cheered up a little as I followed her into the kitchen: at least she was a proper granny in the home-made cake department.

"Tell me about your day," she said, putting a caraway bun and two flapjacks on a plate and pushing it towards me.

"Well," I began, pushing a large piece of bun into my mouth, "there's this school trip, see."

She nodded. "That's nice. To a museum or somewhere, is it?"

I shook my head. "No, it's this awful place where you have to hang-glide and leap off bridges and plunge into waterfalls and generally try to kill yourself."

Granny's eyes gleamed. "How *exciting!*"

I started on the flapjacks. "Yes, well... it's just a pity I won't be able to go."

"Why ever not?"

I thought quickly. "My... bad legs. And my glandular fever." I knew about glandular fever – Georgina had had it all through her exams.

"But you haven't *got* bad legs. And no one mentioned glandular fever to me."

"They didn't want to worry you," I said, eating the other flapjack.

"I'm sure your mum would have mentioned it, dear," Gran said doubtfully. "And what sort of bad legs, anyway?"

"The worst sort," I said promptly.

"But I haven't seen you limping or anything."

I gave a brave smile. "I try and hide it. I don't like to be treated differently from anyone else."

Granny pushed another bun towards me. "Well, I think that an activity holiday like that would probably *help* your glandular fever and your bad legs."

"Oh no it wouldn't!" I said, then added quickly, "I mean, I'd love to be able to go but I just know I wouldn't be able to. I've got to take things easy."

"Well, I'll write to your mother and ask what she thinks."

"No!" I said. "No... er... I'll do it." I grabbed another flapjack and made for my room. "I'll go and do it right now."

"Well, there's one thing to be thankful for," Gran said. I stopped in the doorway, remembering to rub my leg and wince a little. "What's that?"

"At least your glandular fever hasn't ruined your appetite, dear."

I gave a pained smile and went upstairs.

Up in my room – which was Gran's spare room, done out in yukky salmon pink and green – I got out my notepad and prepared for my first shot at getting out of the trip. If it didn't work – well, I had plenty of other ideas up my sleeve.

Dear Mum and Dad, I wrote.

Hope you are well. I am, except that at school they have got this awful trip at the end of term. It's meant to be an adventure holiday but it's terrible and old Wardrobe the gym teacher gets points for the number of broken arms and legs he can make you have.

Well, I'm writing to say that I can't possibly go because I have been feeling really funny lately, exactly like Georgina felt when she had her glandular fever.

I broke off and thought hard here, but I couldn't remember how Georgina *had* felt. She'd just moaned a lot, from what I could remember. And I'd had to do her ironing for her.

I feel sort of moany all the time and can't do any ironing. And another thing is my legs have gone bad. They limp a lot and wouldn't stand the strain of leaping across a ravine.
So please will you write and tell them at school that I can't possibly go.
Write soon. Lots of love, Jane.

P.S. Sorry if my writing is bad but I feel an attack coming on.

CHAPTER THREE

The airmail letter was propped up against my breakfast eggcup just over a week later.

"Your mum's written back very quickly," said Gran.

"I expect she's worried about my legs," I said, tearing open the envelope. I read through her letter quickly: *"What are you talking about darling... never heard such rubbish... you only get glandular fever*

*when you're in your teens... nothing
wrong with your legs except you don't use
them enough... what you need is more
exercise... I'm writing to Gran to say the
school trip sounds the very thing... jolly
good fun..."*

"Well?" Gran asked.

"Er..."

Gran tapped the top of her egg gently.
"Is she writing to school about your
glandular fever, then?"

"Not exactly," I said carefully. "She...
she thinks I'm over the worst of it." I
sighed. It was no good – Gran was getting
a letter anyway. "She thinks I ought to try
and go on the trip," I added dolefully.

"There!" said Gran.

"I just hope she realises what danger she's putting me into."

Gran smiled. "I'm sure she does! Now, how much deposit do you have to take?"

"Don't know," I said. "I've lost the form."

At register that morning Ms Williams was collecting a few stray deposits.

"I think I've got all of your forms back now," she said. She scanned down a list and then peered at me through her big trendy glasses. "Except for yours, Jane."

"That's because I'm not going," I said. There was a gasp and a clatter and rustle as the rest of the class turned round to stare at me. It was as if I'd won the gold ticket to go to the chocolate factory and then announced that I didn't want to go.

"Not going?" "Why not?" "You must be mad!" they all said, and Speedy added, "Trust a girl! S'pose you'd rather stay home and play dollies!"

Everyone sniggered – except Fiona, I was pleased to say. The bell for our first class went and they all jostled to get through the door, still killing themselves laughing. Ms Williams beckoned me over. "Why aren't you going, Jane?" she asked in a kindly and understanding tone.

"I don't want to," I said.

"Is it the... cost?" she asked delicately.

I shook my head. "I just think it sounds awful," I said. "I don't like hang-gliding and swimming and jumping off cliffs and all that sort of thing."

She made a weary tutting noise. "Oh dear, oh dear," she said. "I did hope all the girls in my class had a little more spirit in them than that."

"I just don't like..."

"We're not living in Victorian times! What would you rather do, then – a little light embroidery?"

"No, I..."

But she was off on her high horse, waving her arms around and striding about something alarming. "By playing the weak female you're confirming everything that Mr Ward secretly thinks about us – that we're feeble and ineffective and spend our lives permanently in the shadow of men!"

I took two steps back from this onslaught. "And I've got glandular fever!" I said indignantly.

"Nonsense! I never saw a healthier-looking child in my life. You're a little small perhaps, but that's nothing. Good things come in little packages," she beamed. "Look at me!"

"And my mum said my leg..."

"Your mother will be proud that you've managed to keep up with the boys!" she said. She moved her face so that it was inches from mine. "You go and you show 'em, Jane! There's nothing they can do that we can't, eh!"

"Nothing," I said obediently, for I could see I wasn't going to get anywhere by barking up *this* tree.

I caught up with Fiona in the playground later.

"I've been talking to Speedy," she said.

"Big deal," I said gloomily, wondering

what my friend Manveer would have done. She would have had ten more ideas for getting out of it by now, that was for sure.

"He said that in the whole history of the school..."

"It's only six years old!" I said.

"Yes, well, in the whole six-year-old history of the school, only one boy *hasn't* gone on the school trip."

"Good for him," I said.

"You're supposed to go, see, because it's all part of your primary schooling," she said earnestly. "How you get on at camp goes on your records."

"Well, how did *he* get out of it?" I asked.

"It wasn't that he got out of it – they wouldn't let him go in the first place. He was banned!"

"Oh yes?" I said, suddenly interested. "What did he do?"

"He was so naughty..."

"Yes, but what exactly did he do?"

Her voice fell to a whisper. "That's just it. No one knows for sure. It says on his records, apparently, but it's too terrible to talk about..."

"Wow..." I said, impressed. "So all I've got to do is find his records and then I'll do what he did and I won't be allowed to go either!"

Fiona opened her eyes very wide.

"But... but his records have gone to the Comp with him."

"Then I'll have to go and find them there!" I said. Another idea struck me. "Better still, I'll go and find him! I'll go to the Comp and find him and ask him exactly what he did."

"You wouldn't!"

"Just watch me," I said. "What's his name?"

Fiona looked all round, as if he might be hiding behind the wall or be about to pop out from behind a dustbin. "His name," she said in a fearful voice, "is Killer Matthews."

I stared at her. "K... Killer Matthews," I gulped. "S... sounds a nice boy!"

CHAPTER FOUR

The following week, on Thursday after lunch, I sauntered across the playground of the Comp trying to look as if I belonged there.

I'd planned it all carefully, just like Manveer would have done. The Comp wasn't far from Ridgeway; we could hear them roaring around the place sometimes when the wind was right. All I'd done was to invent an excuse to get out of gym, gone round the back of our sports equipment shed and across our playing field into *their* football field, then round the front of *their* equipment sheds and there I was in the Comp playground.

How I'd act once I'd got there had been planned too. As I'd explained to Fiona, what I mustn't do was skulk in looking scared to death, making it dead obvious that I was an outsider. Instead, I had to *act*.

As I walked across the playground, then, I hummed under my breath, looked nonchalantly around me and swaggered carelessly, just as if I belonged there, as if I was – well, Killer Matthews himself.

I was brilliant; a born actress. *Swagger-swagger... hum-hum* I went, right across the playground clutching my school bag. Their school uniform was almost the same as ours, navy blue and grey, so I didn't reckon I looked that much different from the few stray teenagers loafing about the place.

That week had been ridiculous at Ridgeway. Talk about trip-o-mania, it was all they *talked* about. Wardrobe had put up a big chart on the wall of the gym with each day's activities and you had to sign up and devise a timetable for yourself. The activities were things like rolling a canoe under the water and hoping you came up again or riding a horse bareback and trying to get thrown to the floor and trampled on. Oh, and there was something called murder ball – I didn't want to know what *that* was.

Fiona had supplied me with a description of Killer Matthews – he sounded about as nice as his name. Apparently he was eight feet tall, had red hair shaved at the sides, a ring through his nose and tattoos all up his neck. She'd also found out something about his naughty doings. Speedy King and Tigger said that he'd either flooded the school or burnt part of it down – it wasn't clear which – and had poisoned the canteen food and eaten all the first years' pet animals.

Still, I thought, as I hummed my way across the playground, faced with him or a midnight hike underwater, I'd go for him any day.

"I say!" a plummy voice floated across the playground and a thin lady teacher waved at me to stop.

I gulped. "Yes?" I asked, stopping humming and swaggering.

She came nearer and looked at me severely. "What do you think you're doing out of your class?"

"Delivering a message," I said truthfully.

"For whom?"

I'd prepared myself for this; a good actress should never be without her props. I delved into my pocket and pulled out a piece of paper which I waved about. "For Kill... for Dean Matthews," I said.

She raised her eyebrows. "Then perhaps you should be heading towards the detention block," she said dryly, pointing towards a grey box-like building on stilts. "I believe that's where he spends most afternoons."

"Thank you, miss," I said, turning to go.

"Just a minute!" She clutched me with a bony hand. "Whose class are you in?"

I'd rehearsed this too. A fit of coughing seized me so that I could hardly speak. "Bark... bark... Mrs Mumph-wumph's," I said in a muffled voice, shoving my hand over my mouth and doubling up with racking coughs. "I'm a first year."

"Mrs *whose* class?" she enquired.

I decided to have a fit of sneezing this time – and it was such an explosive, wet sort of fit that it made her step back. "Sorry... sorry," I gasped. "Terrible cold."

She studied me with narrowed eyes. "You don't look quite right, somehow.

Your uniform... your size... yes, that's it. You don't look *old* enough for this school."

I narrowed my shoulders, hunched myself, coughed a pathetic little cough. "That's because I've been very ill," I said. "With this cold and... and glandular fever and other things."

She went right on squinting at me and I decided that I'd have to make it sound better. "The doctor... the doctor feared the worst," I said. "Almost gave me up, he did. I stopped growing for two years, you see."

"Indeed?" she said. "It must have been a severe cold."

I smiled bravely. "I think I'm almost out of it now, miss. Except that I mustn't hang about in draughty playgrounds *if* you'll excuse me..."

With a wistful and ill-looking smile I hurried on towards the grey building on legs that she'd pointed at. When I'd almost reached it I glanced back; she was still standing there, staring. I gave a sneeze loud enough to carry across the playground and disappeared round the corner.

I heaved a loud sigh of relief. Phew! Saved by my remarkable acting abilities.

I skirted the building – it had peeling paint, graffiti and crumbling window frames – then jumped to look through the high windows. Was Killer actually in there? Was he guarded? How long did he have to stay?

"Hey, kid!" Someone seized me by my ankle and I nearly jumped straight out of my blue and grey. Lying in the grass and more under the building than out of it, was a large fair-haired girl eating a jam doughnut. "What you doing here?" she asked aggressively. "You don't go to this school."

"I... I've got a message for Killer," I said nonchalantly.

"Who are you, then?"

I smiled winningly. "I'm a... a friend," I said.

She looked me up and down and burst out laughing, showering me with jam doughnut.

" 'Ere – Killer!" she called further under the building. "You gotta friend to see you!"

There was a growling noise and the grass shifted a little. I froze; I was about to meet Killer...

CHAPTER FIVE

I stared at him in amazement. "Are you...
Killer?" I asked, because the boy who'd
crawled toward me didn't have a tattoo,
an earring or a shaved head. His
reputation had obviously got exaggerated
along the way because, in fact, he looked

quite ordinary; he had fair gingerish hair and was tall and thin. I was relieved, but a bit disappointed too – it was like steeling yourself to come face to face with Tyrannosaurus Rex and only finding a small lizard.

"That's me. In person," he said. As I gawped, the doughnut-eater advanced on me, crawling on all fours. "Want me to see her off, Killer?" she snarled.

"No," Killer said. "Let's see what she wants." He pointed straight above his head. "You'd better get back, anyway. It's about time for Dozer to wake up."

The girl gave me another suspicious look, but nodded. Crouching and crawling, she went further under the building, pulled down a wooden trapdoor and, while I watched open-mouthed, hauled herself upwards and disappeared, shutting the door behind her.

"What's that?" I asked.

"Our escape hatch," Killer said. "We get detention last lesson on most mornings, see, and it gets boring. They only put old Dozer Douglas to watch us, though, and he always goes to sleep, so I got the idea of tunnelling out. We sawed through the floorboards bit by bit and we take it in turns to come down here."

"Fantastic," I said admiringly. "When he wakes up, doesn't he ever notice you're not there, though?"

Killer shrugged carelessly. "Don't think he can count. If someone's out the rest of us just move around a lot." He looked at me. "What d'you want with me then, kid? Don't go to this school, do you?"

I shook my head. "Ridgeway," I said. "Where you used to go." I took a deep breath. "I've come about the school trip; the end-of-year one."

"To that adventure camp?"

I nodded. "I don't want to go on it, you see, but I can't seem to get out of it. Then I heard *you* managed it."

He grinned. "You could put it that way – what actually happened was that they wouldn't let me go."

"Well, however it happened, *you* didn't go and I don't want to, either. I came to ask you what you did so I can do it."

Killer flopped back on the grass. "Phew!" he said. "That's a good few schemes ago." He took a blade of grass and began chewing it. "Now, let's see... it could be the time I ate the goldfish..."

I gave a horrified shriek. "Goldfish, was it? I heard it was the first years' pets. Hamsters, gerbils and white mice, they said. You bit the heads off them."

"Do you mind?" he said. "I'm a vegetarian."

"But eating goldfish is nearly as bad," I pointed out.

"Yeah, well, I didn't exactly eat them,"
he said. "You know that aquarium in
Reception?"

I nodded fearfully.

He grinned. "I floated a few slices of
carrot in there, then, when old Chalky
White was going by, dipped my hand in,
fished them out and chewed them up."

I giggled, relieved. "What happened?"

"Oh, they went mad. They always do."

He looked thoughtful. "Actually, I think it was probably around then that I turned the school mashed potato blue. Maybe that was the reason they wouldn't let me go."

"How did you do that?"

"Easy. Got into the canteen and tipped a bottle of food colouring into the potato vat. But now I think of it, that was after the trip..." He clapped his hand to his head. "No, I remember: it must have been either when I let the sprinklers off or when I hung a pair of knickers on the flagpole. Or maybe it was just everything all in together that got me banned. A sort of job-lot."

I shuddered. "I couldn't climb a flagpole," I said. "I hate heights."

"Let the sprinklers off, then. Or eat a few carrot goldfish."

A bell in the main building of the school began to ring.

"Dinner time," Killer said. "I'd better go. Good luck, kid." He started to crawl towards the trapdoor.

"Can't you stay a bit longer?" I said urgently. "I want to know how the sprinklers work…"

"Nah. Gotta go."

"I thought you said he never noticed when you weren't there?"

As he lowered the trapdoor he shook his head. "It's not that," he said. "I'm not going because of Dozer – I gotta go and open my lunchtime fast food bar. See ya!"

He waved, heaved himself up, and for a moment his grubby trainers dangled from the floor, then he disappeared.

I stared after him for a bit and then, head reeling with ideas, dodged behind sheds and dustbins and portable buildings and made my way back to Ridgeway playground. Fiona was waiting for me by the gate.

She looked at me in awe. "I didn't think you'd come back!" she said as we went into the dining room together. "I thought... I thought he'd *eat* you."

I shrugged airily. "He's all right," I said. "Me and Killer..." I held up two fingers tight together, "like *that*, we are."

"Cr... crumbs" Fiona said.

We got our food from the servery and went to sit down. As we did so, Ms Williams strode to the top platform.

"If you could all just stop eating and talking for a moment..." she said. "I'd like to remind you that, in two weeks' time, we have our annual Grand Jumble Sale." She squinted down the rows of tables. "As most of you will know, we hold the jumble sale to help fund our trip to Tarbeck Gorge. The more money we can raise, the more activities we can provide there! Last year we were able to buy two more sailing dinghies to give all-weather force-ten sailing experience."

I shuddered. Once I'd been sick on a two-minute ferry journey across a river.

"So I'd like you all to start pestering your mums now and begin bringing in your jumble!"

"Oh, I've got loads of things I could bring!" Fiona said as Ms Williams strode off the platform. "All my stuffed toys and loads of games and my last year's summer clothes and..."

I looked at her witheringly. "Do we want this school trip to take place, or don't we?"

She clapped her hand to her mouth. "Sorry. I forgot."

"Anyway, *I* won't be going," I said.
"Not when they find out what I've done."
Fiona's mouth dropped. "What *have* you done?" she asked in a whisper.

"Well, I haven't actually done it yet," I said. "But I know what it'll be..."

"What's that?" she asked fearfully.

"I'm going to turn on the school sprinkler system in the hall," I said, "and half-drown everyone when they're having assembly."

When I looked at Fiona she'd turned quite white. "You wouldn't *really*," she said. "You wouldn't dare."

"Wouldn't I?" I said airily. "Well, put it this way – if I were you I'd wear your anorak to assembly tomorrow morning."

CHAPTER SIX

Holding my breath, I made my way along the corridor to Mr Bright the caretaker's office. It was 8.45 and I should have been in assembly along with the rest of the school, but I had something to do first. I'd found out that the main fire alarm box was in Brightie's storeroom. I just had to smash the glass and press the button inside to set off all the sprinklers in the hall.

Just one press and I wouldn't have to worry about going on the stupid school trip any more – and with a bit of luck Brightie would be out doing his rounds. I was going to creep in there, smash the glass, press the red button and...

"Just a minute, dear." A hand landed on my shoulder and I stopped in my tracks. I looked up into the face of the school nurse, known as Fat Annie. She had a big,

powdered face and budgie-blue
eyeshadow. "It's little Jane, isn't it?"

I nodded, staring at her stonily. I didn't
care that I'd been seen – I wanted
everyone to know it was me who'd set the
sprinklers off – but I hated being called
little.

"I was coming to see your granny
tonight, dear," she said. Her face was
inches from mine and she spoke slowly

and caringly. "I understand you're living with her at the moment."

"That's right," I muttered.

"Well, I'm the school welfare assistant as well as your nurse," she said, "and I want to have a word with Granny about the school trip." I carried on staring and she went on, "Ms Williams tells me that you're the only one who hasn't paid."

I thought fast. It wouldn't be bad to have a fall-back plan in case the sprinklers didn't go off. I shook my head sadly. "Granny can't afford the money," I said, "so I'm afraid I won't be going with the other lucky children."

She smiled so caringly that the eyeshadow got swallowed up by her eyes. "But couldn't your parents pay, dear?"

I blinked several times, working myself up for a nice bit of acting. "My parents... my mummy and daddy... are... are gone," I gulped.

Her face loomed over me, large and moon-like. She pushed her hand up to her mouth as if to stifle a cry. "Oh, my *dear!* You mean... actually *gone?*"

I nodded, looked upwards to heaven and pointed with a quivering finger. "Gone... gone far away into the sky."

"No! I had no idea. How terrible..."

I brushed away an imaginary tear, not even bothering to cross my fingers. Well, it was all perfectly true – they'd gone on a DCl0 from Heathrow.

Her face became a mask of tragedy. She clasped me to her starched front; my face pressed into her watch. "Forgive me for mentioning it... how sad... we must do something... a poor orphan... Social Services must be told..."

Struggling for air, I wriggled and squirmed. "Must go; late for assembly," I spluttered. I managed to get out of her clutches and walked, shoulders sagging tragically, to the corner. Once round it, I broke into a run. I had to get on with the job before everyone came out of the hall.

The next bit was easy. There was no one in the storeroom, and on the wall were the electricity meters and various other switches and bits and pieces – and a great red box with a glass front and a big red button inside.

I gritted my teeth, just a little bit scared. Did I really dare? I'd never *ever* done anything even half-way *that* bad before. Suppose I was expelled? I suddenly brightened... if I was, then I *definitely* couldn't go on the trip.

I took off my shoe, took a deep breath, closed my eyes and smashed the glass – then nearly leapt two feet in the air when the loudest bells I've ever heard began shrieking out.

I put out my hand and looked up, but there was no water showering down on

me, just bells, piercing bells, horrible shrieky bells. I then noticed another red alarm box further along from the one I'd hit. I'd got the wrong box!

I put my head out of the store room – there was no one about – and began to run along the corridor toward the school hall.

"Stop thief!"

As I turned the corner and went past the computer room and the library, there was a crash and then Brightie suddenly lumbered past me with his brown coat flapping, roaring and bellowing above the bells. "Stop him, someone! He's got our new computers!" he yelled.

I stared after Brightie in amazement; what *was* he going on about? As he passed the hall where assembly was still going on, the double doors were flung open and a horde of kids ran out, shouting and yelling, closely followed by Wardrobe.

"There he goes, sir!" someone shrieked, pointing out of an open window, and Wardrobe jumped straight through it, tore across the playground and rugby-tackled a man I'd never seen before – a man who was wheeling a trolley full of computers. Wardrobe brought him down on the ground to loud cheers.

It was all chaos after that. Dead exciting. All the kids did a sort of war-dance round the thief, then the police came, then we all went back into assembly where Chalky

White got serious and asked who'd set the alarm bells going.

I stood up. This was it. Goodbye school...

"It was me," I said. "Jane Howard."

"Well!" he said. "Our new girl, isn't it?"

"Yes," I said, "and I did it because I..."

"Because you saw the thief! Well done, Jane!"

"No, because I..."

"You showed a great deal of initiative. You saw the thief, ran into the storeroom and sounded that alarm straight away. You are to be congratulated. If Mr Bright hadn't heard the alarm he wouldn't have been alerted, and then computers worth several thousand pounds would have been stolen!"

I coughed uneasily. "Well, I..."

"And if those computers *had* been stolen, let me tell you that the school trip would have been in jeopardy."

An alarmed muttering broke out right across the hall, but from 10A especially.

"Our priority would have been to replace them from school funds and then there wouldn't have been enough for our top class to go to Tarbeck Gorge at the end of term."

While I stood in stunned silence, one of the teachers started clapping me and everyone else joined in. Fat Annie wiped away a tear.

"Thanks to you, Jane, the computers – and the school trip – have been saved!" Ms Williams shouted. "Come on, everyone: *For she's a jolly good fellow, for she's a jolly good fellow...*"

Wearing the sickest sort of smile, I sat down.

"Aren't you clever!" Fiona said, clapping me on the back.

"Oh yeah. Just brilliant," I said.

CHAPTER SEVEN

"Now, I've sorted out a nice lot of jumble for you to take to school on Saturday," Gran said when I came home from school a week or so later.

I frowned deeply over my slice of strawberry shortcake. "How did you know there was going to be a jumble sale?"

"The newsletter!" she said, holding up a piece of paper. "I found it screwed up in the bottom of your school bag."

"Oh," I said, pulling a face and popping in a gooseberry turnover. I thought I'd chucked that letter away.

"It says here that all proceeds from the jumble sale will go towards the trip to Tarbeck Gorge," Gran read out. "That's nice, isn't it?"

"Great," I said, working my brain along with my jaws. Time was running out fast... there were only three weeks to go. Gran had paid for me now – sent a cheque to school – so there was no hope of pretending that we couldn't afford it. I knew that the trip was only partly paid for by the parents, though, so maybe if no money came in from the jumble sale...

That was it! The jumble sale would have to be stopped. Somehow I'd have to try and get in to the school secretary's office and do some *"Unfortunately, owing to unforeseen circumstances, the jumble sale has had to be cancelled"* letters. But how would I get them round the school without a teacher seeing, and what...

Just as I was planning what my next move would be, the front door bell rang. I went – Gran was just getting a batch of home-made goodies out of the oven.

"Eeek!" I said when I opened the door, for Fat Annie stood there taking up most of the doorway. She was wringing her hands, deep concern written all over her face. "Dearie..." she said heavily.

"Yes?" I asked, pulling the door shut behind me so that Gran wouldn't hear.

"I've come to ask how you are," she said, her voice dripping with sympathy, "and to see if there's anything the school can do for our poor little..."

"Nothing at all, thank you," I said briskly.

"But since your mother and father are... since... well, you're an *orphan*, dear..."

I coughed loudly. "Got to go," I said. "Poor Granny and I are... er... boiling up some old crusts to make soup."

"Who is it, Jane?" came Gran's voice.

"No one!" I called, but before I could say anything else, Gran appeared behind me. "Someone from school, is it?"

Fat Annie gave her the full disappearing-eye smile and Gran stepped back, startled.

"I'm the nurse from Jane's school," she said heavily, "and I just came to see how the poor little thing was coping with the... the terrible tragedy."

Gran looked at her blankly. As well she might. "What tragedy's that, then?"

"Nurse means... means Mum and Dad... *going*," I said in a strangled voice.

Gran nodded. "Oh, that," she said dismissively. "Well, it's not so bad, Nurse," she said. "You've got to look at it from their point of view, you see. What I say is that it makes a nice change for them."

Fat Annie looked startled. "That's... er... one way of looking at it, I suppose."

"And we've got used to it without them, haven't we, Jane? In fact, we sometimes prefer it."

I gave a sickly smile and a nod and Fat Annie looked surprised, then a bit outraged.

"But do come in," Gran went on. "It's not often we get visitors."

"I'm sure Fa... Nurse is really busy," I said quickly. "We mustn't keep..."

But she was already in the kitchen, staring at the strawberry shortcake and goggling at the gooseberry turnovers.

"No, it's not so bad," Gran repeated. "and there are the letters, of course."

"L... letters?" Fat Annie asked, even more startled.

Gran gestured to the airmail letters from Mum on the mantelpiece. "Once a week, regular."

"But I didn't think... I mean... how on earth do they...?"

"Oh, it's marvellous what they can do nowadays with the mail," Gran said. "Even from ever so far away."

Very slowly, I started to move towards the door.

"Did they go... suddenly?" Fat Annie asked delicately. "I mean – both of them together, sort of thing?"

"Oh yes," Gran said blithely. "Both together. Tourist class, two for the price of one, as I recall."

I felt behind me for the door handle.

"It's *very* very hot where they are, of course," Gran went on. "Couldn't stand it myself."

"Very... hot... " Fat Annie echoed faintly.
"Not a place I'd choose to go..."

"But you don't. Choose, I mean," said
Fat Annie.

"Oh, you can nowadays. I mean, they
could have gone there or Australia – but
Jane's dad is frightened of kangaroos and
Jane's mum can't stand Rolf Harris, so
that was right out."

"*Rolf Harris?*" Fat Annie panted. "But
is... but really... I don't..."

Softly, very softly, I opened the door and
crept upstairs.

CHAPTER EIGHT

"Now, you get hold of that end and start untying it!" I called to Fiona. She was sitting on one of the stone pillars by the school gates, and I was on the opposite one.

"Are you sure we're not going to be seen?" she said worriedly, looking up and down the road.

"No, I'm not sure," I said, "so *hurry.*"

We were perched on the wall like two stone ornaments, holding the ends of the huge *"Jumble Sale Today At Two O'Clock"* banner which ran across the gateway, and trying to untie them.

I hadn't managed to send out any *"Unfortunately the jumble sale is cancelled"* letters, but, without the advertising banner and with a bit of luck, only a few people would turn up at two o'clock. And then, when they did, they wouldn't find much jumble.

Brightie, you see, had gone off alarming about the risk of fire if the jumble was kept in the school, so he was only allowing the school hall to be opened for jumble at one o'clock. People had to bring in their jumble then and have it sorted by me and Fiona and a few others... and I planned to get as much out of the hall as I possibly could. I intended to go backwards and forwards, home and back, dressed in ten jumpers and half a dozen coats at a time.

If there was no jumble then there would be nothing to buy – and if there was nothing to buy then the Tarbeck Gorge School Trip Fund wouldn't get any money.

There were only two weeks to go before the off and I was fast running out of ideas. Since the fuss I'd got into with Fat Annie and Gran I'd been lying low for a bit, but I'd decided that sabotaging the jumble sale was at least worth a try. If it didn't work, then I had one more thing up my sleeve, and if that failed then I'd have a quick last-minute go at catching a disease the Friday afternoon before we went.

JUMBLE SALE TODAY AT 2 o'clock

We managed to get the banner off at last – I had to climb Fiona's pillar in the end and help her – and then I rolled it up into a ball and struggled home with it. I went back to school at midday; I was determined to get into that hall before anyone else.

Taking my life into my hands, I knocked on the door of Brightie's house – he lived just a playground's width away from the school.

He opened the door, looked me up and down and scowled at me – he didn't really go with his name.

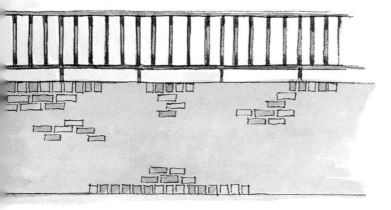

"I'm just having me dinner," he said crossly. "What d'you want?"

"Sorry I'm so early," I said charmingly. "I just thought I'd save you the bother of walking to the school to open up."

"What you on about?" he asked, wiping his mouth with the back of his hand.

"I thought I could take the key and open up the hall for you to save you the trouble," I said. "You could have a nice snooze after your dinner then."

He eyed me suspiciously. "Going straight out to football after I've eaten," he said.

"Well, then," I said, "if I take the key you'll be able to get to the match all the quicker." I smiled winningly. "I don't think it's fair that you should be asked to work Saturdays anyway, do you?"

"No, I don't!" he said.

"So I'll bring the key straight back, Mr Bright... take really good care of it," I said earnestly. "You can rely on me."

"Well..." he said.

"I was just saying the other day how *very* hard you work. If I may say so, our hall floor absolutely *gleams*."

He turned away from the door to a line of hooks behind him. "You bring the key straight back, then. If I'm out, put it through the letter box."

"Oh, I will," I said. He handed it over and I clasped it to me just as if I'd been given the crown jewels.

I hurried back to school to open up – and then, just as I was about to do so, had another, even more brilliant idea. What if, come Jumble Sale time, the hall *wasn't open?* What if everyone turned up with their jumble and had to go home? What if, in other words, the key had been mislaid...?

A couple of hours later, by the time Ms Williams arrived, I'd repeated my story so many times that I was beginning to believe it. "Well, you see, I went and collected the key to the school hall to save poor Mr Bright's legs and then I sort of tripped – my legs keep going funny lately – and the key flew out of my hand and I can't find it anywhere! And the terrible thing is, Mr Bright has gone out for the afternoon so we can't get a spare."

"But this is ridiculous!" Ms Williams said. "We've got all these people waiting around with their jumble and there's nowhere to put it!"

"I know," I said, trying hard to look more concerned and less gleeful.

"And where's our advertising banner that's supposed to be over the gateway?" she added indignantly. "I'm going to have a strong word with Mr Bright when I see him."

Beside me, Fiona gave a frightened squeak.

"It was there earlier," I said quickly.

"There's been a strong wind, though. Perhaps it blew away."

"Not very likely," Ms Williams said. "Oh dear – there's another three cars arriving with jumble. I'd better go and speak to them."

She went towards them and then she suddenly stopped and clapped her hand to her mouth. "Of *course*," she said. "I've got it!"

"What's that?" I said. "I don't think we ought to force our way into the..."

"We can't have a jumble sale – but we *can* have a car boot sale!"

"Oh, what a good idea!" Fiona said, and I poked her hard in the ribs.

"All the cars can come into the playground and sell their stuff from there. We'll charge £5 per car and they can keep half the money they make!"

"Oh, but... um... I don't..." I began, but no one was listening to me, they were all rushing about telling everyone else and excitedly spreading the news.

The cars started coming in, someone went home and made a couple of cardboard placards saying "GRAND CAR BOOT SALE NOW ON!!!" and propped them up against the gates, and people got out of their cars and started buying things from other people's cars.

Some of those who'd come on foot with their jumble doubled up in other people's cars, others went home and got their own. Passing strangers, seeing all the action, drove home, piled their cars with jumble and came back again.

"I'd never go to a jumble sale – but a car boot sale's different!" a woman beamed at me, pushing a five pound note into my hand.

"*Such* a good idea of mine," Ms Williams said, whipping the money out of my hand smartish and putting it in a tin.

"I'm so glad you mislaid the key, Jane!"

"I just can't believe it!" she said an hour or so later. "We've never taken so much. Do you realise that we've doubled the money we usually make from jumble sales?"

"Fancy..." I said, with the sickly smile that I couldn't seem to stop smiling recently.

She gave a hearty laugh. "Why, we could almost afford to send you all to Tarbeck Gorge for two weeks instead of one! Wouldn't that be great, eh?"

"That," I said dourly, "would be just about perfect."

CHAPTER NINE

"I'll do it," I said, putting my hand up straight away. "I'll go and help."

Everyone in the class turned to stare – especially Speedy King, who pulled a face at me as well.

"You, Jane?" Ms William asked in surprise. "You're actually offering to go and help Mr Ward to type the Tarbeck Gorge equipment lists?"

I nodded, acting indignant. "I can *do* it, you know," I said. "I do know how to use the keyboard on a computer."

"Of course you do," Ms Williams said, "I was just surprised that you wanted to help. I didn't think you were all that keen on anything to do with the trip."

I gave her my sunniest smile. "Oh, that was *ages* ago."

Ms Williams nodded. "I knew once you realised what *fun* it was all going to be...

why, once you get there you'll be running down ravines and tightrope-walking across canyons with the best of them!"

"Of course," I said. But they had to get me there first.

I stood up. "Shall I go along to the computer room now?"

"If you would," she said. She looked at her watch. "And then you can come back here and distribute the lists to everyone before lunch." She raised a fist in the air. "Just one more week before the Great Adventure begins, eh, everyone?"

There was an answering roar from the class and I bent down to pick up my bag.

"What d'you want to go and help Wardrobe for?" Fiona asked in a whisper. "What are you up to now?"

"Something good," I said. "You'll see."

Wardrobe was hunched into a chair in the computer room and typing very slowly, one key at a time. He was so big he dwarfed the computer and overhung his chair on each side – he looked a bit like one of those experiments to see what a gorilla can do on a typewriter.

"I've come to help you, sir," I said.

He looked round. "Ahh... good!" he said. "Just the sort of person I need. My fingers are too big for these keys – whenever I press one letter, three appear."

"You can leave it to me, sir," I said in a goody-goody voice. "Tell me what you want done and then you can go off and do some more kicking people... er... rugby or whatever."

"Right!" he said, and he thrust a piece of paper at me. "Here's my list of what each child will need at Tarbeck. If you can type it I'll come back and print it out."

"No need, sir," I said. "We've done some work on these and I can do it myself. And when they're printed I'll take them back to class and give them out."

He beamed at me and went to clap me on the shoulder, but I dodged just in time.

"Jolly good!" he said, lumbering towards the door. "And to show how grateful I am, when we get to Tarbeck I'll see you have first go at the new high-speed para-glider! How about that?"

"Oh, great, sir!" I said. I was getting brilliant at acting, just brilliant...

I shut the door firmly behind him and looked down at the sheet he'd given me.

List of Essential Equipment for Tarbeck
Gorge:
Two pairs of jeans.
One waterproof anorak.
Wellington boots.
Waterproof over-trousers.
T-shirts.
Warm jumpers for night trekking.
Waterproof sheet for sleeping out
overnight (note: sleeping bags can be
borrowed from Tarbeck Gorge).
Trainers (two pairs for wet and dry
activities).
Rucksack.
Small amount of dehydrated food.
Water flask.
Sturdy gloves suitable for rope work.

I read through it twice, thinking deeply. This was the essential equipment list – so all I had to do was make up a new one containing things which no one's parents could possibly obtain, and then no one would be able to go...

Smirking to myself, I typed:

List of Essential Equipment for Tarbeck Gorge:

(Note: No child will be allowed on the coach without everything (and I mean everything) on this list. If you can't get everything, don't bother to send your child.)

Eight pairs of jeans.

One full-length (down to the ground) waterproof coat.

Thigh-length wellington boots.

Six pairs of waterproof over-trousers.

T-shirts (must be pale green with design showing lambs leaping around the neck).

Warm jumpers made of 100% angora rabbit combings for night trekking (must be orange).

Waterproof sheet for sleeping out

overnight. (Note: sleeping bags are not available for hire so must be bought in advance. Have to be striped yellow and green and filled with curled duck feathers.)
Eighteen pairs of trainers.
Six rucksacks.
Pre-skinned rabbit in case supplies of food dry up.
Small pan suitable for frying worms.
Surgical gloves for carrying out operations on each other.

This done (it took ages) I stared at my new list, well pleased with it. I wondered briefly about adding an electric drill, decided that might be going too far, and then pressed the help key to try to work out how to print.

The computer was user-friendly so this turned out to be a piece of cake. All was going well and I was up to copy number twenty-seven when Wardrobe crashed through the door, causing me to almost leap in the air with fright.

"Nearly finished, Jane?"

"Er..." I hastily stood up and draped myself in front of the screen.

"Let's have a look, then!"

"I'd rather you didn't, sir," I said nervously. "I'd like it to be a surprise."

"I'm too old for surprises," he said. I had a quick go at falling on to the keyboard and trying to erase everything, but it didn't work. He moved me away with one finger, sat down on the chair and stared at the screen.

"Jumpers of angora rabbit combings... sleeping bags with curled duck feathers... frying worms... surgical gloves..." His voice got higher and higher the more he read out. He looked at me in amazement. "What on earth – have you had a brainstorm or something?"

I coughed uneasily. "Well, er... I thought your list was a bit boring, so I added a few..."

To my surprise, he began to roar with laughter. "Jolly good... jolly good!" he said. "But where's the real list?"

"I haven't actually..."

He pointed to my newly-printed pile. "Don't tell me you've wasted all that paper, Jane."

"Umm..."

His eyebrows furrowed together. "Well, you'll just have to use the back of these printed lists – and you'll have to write them by hand; there's a group booked on the computers in three minutes time."

"*What?*"

"It'll be a bit like writing lines, Jane: thirty copies of the *real* Tarbeck Gorge equipment list, please. And don't leave anything out. You can carry on through your lunchtime too."

"But *sir...*" I protested.

"I'll be back later to see how you're getting on!" he said cheerfully. "Keep at it!"

Sighing deeply, I reached for the pile of printed sheets and turned them over. Grudgingly, resentfully, I began to write: "*List of Essential Equipment for Tarbeck Gorge.*"

And there was only a week to go...

CHAPTER TEN

"I think I've got measles," I said to Gran. It was Tarbeck Gorge departure day and I was standing in Gran's hall next to my rucksack containing every single thing on the equipment list (official version). "I think I ought to go back to bed."

"You've *had* measles," she said.

"Well, German measles, then. Or chicken pox or something." I looked at myself in the hall mirror and pushed hard at my cheek. "Look, there's a huge red mark there."

"I expect there is," Gran said cheerily, "considering you've been poking your cheek all through breakfast."

"You don't care, do you?" I sighed heavily. "When I come back from Tarbeck Gorge *dead* you'll be sorry."

"I expect so, dear – but at least I'll be able to rent out your room."

I looked at her bitterly. "I'm going upstairs to clean my teeth," I said, "and if I feel faint with chicken pox and fall into the sink and drown then I might not come down again."

In the bathroom I cleaned my teeth slowly and thoroughly, racking my brains for further dregs of ideas. What would Manveer have done? I bet she'd have been able to think of something...

I looked mournfully at my reflection in the mirror. None of my ideas had worked... and in an hour's time I'd be on my way to six days of absolute misery and if not certain death – well, some terrible injury at the very *least*.

I wiped my mouth and then stood at the top of the stairs, wondering whether to throw myself down them. What would be the good of that, though? I'd only break my leg – which was exactly what I was trying to avoid by getting out of the trip. Besides, carrying out ideas and schemes was one thing, but being brave enough to crash down the stairs was quite another. I didn't *dare*.

"Come on!" Gran called. "I want to walk up to school with you and see you off."

I went down. "As it'll probably be the last you see of me, you'd better take a good look."

She snorted in an ungrannylike way. "Now, I've got a nice big tin of flapjacks here; you can take them along for a midnight feast."

"Huh!" I said, pulling on my anorak and struggling to get the rucksack on my back. "We'll be out all night crawling on our stomachs through swamps, there won't be any time for midnight feasts. Besides, when we get back the wolves will have eaten all our provisions."

"Jolly clever wolves who can open tins!" Gran said.

Up at school, all was bustle and excitement. None of the rest of the school had gone in – they were all waiting to see us off – and there was a large blue coach parked in the playground with

"Destination: Tarbeck Gorge" on the front. Speedy King, Tigger and his mates were running round and round in excited circles, while Wardrobe strode about waving a clipboard, patting children on the head and sending them flying. Ms Williams, wearing what looked like a wet suit without the flippers, barked out instructions and shouted at parents to *please* put their children in line so that they could be counted.

"All right?" Fiona asked, arriving beside me bowed down under a green rucksack.

"Not really," I said.

"I mean... well, it's quite exciting now that we're actually going, isn't it? Maybe it's going to be all right."

"Of course it isn't," I said. "It's going to be absolutely awful. Besides, I'm not there yet. Anything could happen..."

"Ooh, you don't mean to say you're still..."

An idea suddenly struck me and I left her and Gran – who was talking to Fiona's mum – and went over to Wardrobe.

"Sir!" I caught hold of his arm. "Could I have a word, please?"

"What is it, Jane? Glandular fever – or is it your legs again?"

"Neither, sir," I said with dignity. "I have got a touch of chicken pox, actually, but no one believes me. No, what I wanted to say was, I don't think I'll be able to go because of leaving my old gran."

He raised one eyebrow. "Oh yes? And what's wrong with your old gran?"

"She... she's gone a bit ga-ga," I said earnestly. "Do-lally, if you know what I mean. She doesn't know which way up she is. And she relies on me for everything now – to do the shopping and cooking and all. She can't manage on her own any more."

"What – she's in a wheelchair, is she?" I nodded, crossing my fingers. "She can only move her nose. Dead pitiful it is, sir. She twitches it once for yes, twice for no."

"But Jane," Wardrobe said, "isn't that your gran talking to Fiona's mum? Isn't she the little lady laughing her head off – the one with the big tin of what looks like home-made goodies under her arm?"

I looked where he was pointing, and rubbed my eyes in feigned astonishment.

"Crumbs!" I said in wonderment. "I... I just don't believe it! It... it's..."

"A miracle, obviously," he said dryly.

"Yes!" I said.

He patted me on the head and I sank several inches into the ground. "You ought to be an actress, Jane. In fact, I'll do you a reference for drama school any time." He consulted his clipboard. "Talking of which... one thing I didn't realise before – this year there's a new activity at Tarbeck Gorge."

"Oh yes?" I said dolefully. "What is it – roasting people over a spit? Pushing people over the rapids without a barrel?"

"No," he said. "They've recognised that not all children want to partake in mad outdoor activities, so there's a travelling theatre group there."

I stared at him. "What?"

"Instead of adventuring about you can do a week's drama course – and at the end of your time there you put on a play which the whole camp watches."

"Oh," I said.

"They've particularly asked me to let them have the names of any children who show an aptitude for drama, so if you like... still, if you're worried about Gran – and if your chicken pox is going to develop any further..."

"It's finished," I said quickly. "I had it last week but it's gone, and Gran..." I looked over towards where she seemed to be demonstrating the hornpipe to Fiona's mum, "...will probably be all right now that the miracle's happened."

"Well, the drama course it is, then," he said briskly. "That's you settled."

Ms Williams ran up waving her clipboard. "Frightening my girls to death again, Mr Ward?"

"Just a little!" Wardrobe said, grinning.

She gave me a bracing smile, "I don't think it'll be quite as bad as you think there, Jane." She tapped her watch.

"Anyway, it's time to be off," she said. "Let's get everyone on the coach and do a final head-count."

I left them and sped back to Gran and Fiona. "Come on!" I said to Fiona breathlessly. "We've got to go!"

Fiona looked at me. "What have you done *now?*" she said. "Let down the coach tyres?"

I looked at her in surprise. Why hadn't I thought of that? "Course not!" I said.

"What, then? You're not going to throw yourself off the coach halfway there, are you? Or run away, or..."

"No, no... none of those," I said impatiently. "Come on, then we can get seats together on the coach."

I kissed Gran, Fiona kissed her mum, and then we went across the playground together.

"What have you done?" she persisted. "You might at least tell me."

"Nothing to tell," I said as we climbed aboard. "It's just that I've been specially selected as chief actress of Tarbeck Gorge and I'm going to have the starring role in the play."

She screwed up her face. "What are you talking about?"

Just as I was going to explain and to say that she could have a smaller acting role, Ms Williams jumped on the coach, clapping her hands for silence. "We want to get away on time, because the school that gets there first gets the best dorms!"

"Didn't know there were any other schools going," I said to Fiona.
She nodded. "There always are."

"This year," Ms Williams went on, "there's a large group from Cornwall and also the top class of a new school who've never been before from..." she consulted a sheet of paper, "...Salisbury. Rivermead School, Salisbury."

I clutched Fiona, almost speechless.
"What's the matter?"

"My old school!" I croaked. "It's my old class from my old school! Manveer and Mandy and Anna and all my friends!"

She turned to stare at me, eyes wide with amazement, and I settled myself back in my seat, opened Gran's cake tin and passed it along. "I think," I said slowly, "that I *might* be going to enjoy Tarbeck Gorge after all..."